THE BROWNIE VENTURERS

'*Could we have a Venture? An exciting sort of one?*'

Brown Owl asked the pack what they would like to do.

'*Go on a picnic,*' *suggested Joan. Ideas began to come.*

'*Have a fete and sell things for Pack Funds.*'

'*Have an entertainment and ask our parents.*'

'*A jumble sale.*'

'*A coffee morning ...*'

'*No, that's too ordinary,*' *Hilary interrupted a little scornfully,* '*it should be something exciting.*'

None of the Brownies has come up with a really good idea, when a hidden message leads them to a ready-made Venture – with some surprising results.

About the author

Dorothy Richardson was born and brought up in Ireland, but she has lived in England for over twenty years. She used to run her own Brownie Pack in Northwood, just outside London.

Dorothy Richardson has contributed articles and short stories to magazines including *The Brownie Magazine*, *Child Education* and *Teacher's World*. She has written a number of other books about Brownies.

Knight Books publish the following Brownie titles:

Verily Anderson
THE BROWNIE COOKBOOK
THE BROWNIES AND THE CHRISTENING
THE BROWNIES AND THEIR ANIMAL FRIENDS
THE BROWNIES' DAY ABROAD
THE BROWNIES AND THE WEDDING DAY
BROWNIES ON WHEELS

Dorothy Richardson
THE SECRET BROWNIES
THE BROWNIE RESCUERS

The Brownie Venturers

Dorothy Richardson

Illustrated by Thelma Lambert

KNIGHT BOOKS
Hodder and Stoughton

Copyright © Dorothy Richardson 1982
Illustrations copyright © Hodder & Stoughton Ltd 1982

First published by Hodder & Stoughton
Children's Books 1982

Knight Books edition 1983
Third impression 1985

British Library C.I.P.

Richardson, Dorothy
 The Brownie Venturers.
 I. Title
823´.914[J]   PZ7

 ISBN 0 340 32887 8

Printed and bound in Great Britain for Hodder and
Stoughton Paperbacks, a division of Hodder and
Stoughton Ltd., Mill Road, Dunton Green, Sevenoaks,
Kent (Editorial Office: 47 Bedford Square, London, WC1
3DP) by Cox & Wyman Ltd, Reading

Chapter 1

Maureen was dancing her way over the buttercups that grew like a golden carpet in the field near the Brownie hut. She hated to squash any of the shining flowers so she went on tip-toe, hopping over the blooms. This meant she was making very slow progress, but as she had left home even earlier than usual, there was plenty of time.

When she came to the fallen tree trunk she sat astride it for a moment, imagining it was a magic horse that galloped over the buttercup carpet without so much as making a hoof mark on the flowers, and landed her at the hut in time for pack meeting. It would be exciting to arrive at the hut by magic horse. Just then, she remembered something Miss Atkins had said just after she became their new Brown Owl. The fun of being 'Secret' Brownies had come to an end and they were all feeling a little bit sorry. But then Maureen had remarked, hopefully, 'There'll probably be other exciting things ahead.' 'Of course there will,'

Miss Atkins had replied, 'All we need is plenty of ideas.'

She wished she could think of a really exciting idea, one that might lead on to an adventure, one that she could make into a story for her Writer Badge. Perhaps they could have a Venture at Brownies, a different sort of one. She'd suggest it at Pow-Wow if she got the chance. Hilary was the one who always seemed to have the ideas, this time *she'd* have one.

'Maureen, Maur —' She looked round sharply to see Valerie running across the field towards her, her mouth open and her face pink. Though she was small and plump and not a good runner, she moved over the grass faster than Maureen had done because she wasn't worrying about the buttercups, in fact she didn't notice they were there.

'I thought you'd never hear me, I kept shouting.' She reached the tree trunk and leaned against it, pulling a packet of fruit gums from her uniform pocket. One had already stuck to the inside of her pocket and made a mess.

'Here, have one, I've got to finish them because we're having a pocket inspection this evening and I don't want Brown Owl to see them. I've got everything else.'

She pulled a piece of string, a fivepence piece, an envelope with a hanky in it, a safety pin and a notebook and pencil out of her pocket and laid them on the tree trunk.

'Oh, I'd forgotten about that,' said Maureen, 'I was just wondering.' She stopped as she sometimes did in the middle of a sentence. Valerie stared at her. When Maureen was in one of her dreamy moods she went off into a world she couldn't share with anyone, and Valerie felt left out.

'Oh, all right then.' She popped the last fruit gum into her mouth and gathered up the items she had laid out. 'We'd better get on.'

'M-mm'. Maureen slid reluctantly off the tree trunk and they set off together. On the way she asked Valerie if she had an exciting idea. Valerie hadn't. But she thought she would like to be included in a Venture if they had one.

Pack meeting was about to start as they arrived. Hilary, the Kelpie sixer, was getting her six into position for the Brownie Ring ceremony and the Song. Later, towards the end of the meeting, they all sat on the floor for a Pow-Wow. Hilary was usually first to speak so Maureen quickly got her suggestion in first.

'Could we have a Venture? An exciting sort of one?'

Brown Owl asked the pack what they would like to do.

'Go on a picnic,' suggested Joan. Ideas began to come.

'Have a fete and sell things for Pack Funds.'

'Have an entertainment and ask our parents.'

'A jumble sale.'

'A coffee morning and sell cakes,' said Mary. 'My Mum makes super cakes and so does Aunt Helen, last week she made a coffee one for the Women's Institute Country Market and Mum made lemon buns and I helped her. I can make fairy cakes and biscuits and —'

'No, that's too ordinary,' Hilary interrupted a little scornfully, 'it should be something exciting.'

'That *is* exciting,' Mary retorted. How was it that Hilary always thought *her* ideas the best? And she had spoken without first making their special sign of two fingers placed on the floor in front of her.

She was about to speak again when Brown Owl said quickly, knowing how Mary sometimes went on and on,

'They're all possibilities, let's think about them before next week.'

She looked at the clock on the wall.

'It's time to finish, bring any more ideas to next meeting and we can decide then.'

The pack stood up for Brownie Bells.

Outside the Brownie hut, Hilary drew some of the others into a little group before they set off for home. There was Joan, her Second, Maureen, who was the Pixie Sixer, and two other members of Maureen's Six, Mary and Valerie, together with Peggy and Pat Martin, sisters, who were in the Elves.

'Let's meet somewhere and get an idea for a really good Venture before next pack meeting.'

'Where?' asked Valerie.

'You know that tree at the entrance to the stables when they belonged to the Manor?' asked Hilary. 'We could meet there.'

'Yes, the one in the footpath field,' said Peggy,

'the way we used to go when we met in the coach house.'

'The stables are being turned into flatlets for old people now,' Hilary reminded them.

They decided to meet under the tree after school on Monday.

Hilary and Joan were first to arrive, closely followed by Maureen. The sound of hammering and banging rose above the cawing of the rooks in the tree. The flatlets, or bungalows, were well under way. They could see that the old clock on the tower rising above the roofs had been left there. Now it told the correct time.

Hilary grasped a lower branch of the tree and swung her feet off the ground, while Joan squatted down on the grass under the tree and hugged her knees, Maureen beside her.

'Here's Val, and Mary.'

Valerie was sucking a sweet as usual. She was panting and found it too hard to keep up with Mary. They were followed by Peggy and Pat, the fastest runners in the Pack, who soon outdistanced the other two.

'Has anyone got an idea for an exciting Venture?' asked Hilary as soon as they had all arrived.

'Let's make it something to help people,' suggested Maureen.

'The wheelchair children,' Mary was thinking of their friends at the hospital whom they had helped when they were 'Secret' Brownies.

Pat knelt down under the tree. She placed her head on the ground, then slowly raised her legs in

the air, her clasped hands and bent elbows forming a triangle around her head. She straightened her legs and placed her feet against the tree trunk.

Peggy gazed at her sister admiringly.

'That's good Pat, hold it!'

'Hush, I'm thinking,' Pat's voice sounded different, 'and I think better like this, I've been practising.'

'*I* didn't know,' Peggy sounded astonished.

'You don't know everything,' Pat retorted sharply as she bent her knees, lowered her legs and came upright again. Usually, she followed Peggy in everything she did, but lately she had begun to do things on her own.

'And I've seen something nobody else has.'

'Where?' asked Hilary.

They all followed Pat's gaze as she pointed up into the lower branches of the tree.

'What's that?'

Sticking out of a small hollow not far above their heads was a screw top jar with something white inside it.

'Let me see.' Hilary put up an arm, but it was just out of her reach.

'Give me a hoist up,' said Peggy, clinging like a monkey to the tree trunk while holding on to a small branch with one hand.

Pat took one leg while Hilary clasped the other

and slowly they raised her higher. Her hand reached the jar and grasped it.

'I've got it.'

They lowered her legs, letting go too soon so that she slithered down, scraping her knees and hands and dropping the jar.

'Ow!'

'Hilary pounced on the jar and opened it.

While Peggy was rubbing her knees and wondering whether to make a fuss about them or not, Pat grabbed the jar.

'I saw it first.'

'Yes she did.' Peggy forgot about her knees and stood up for her sister.

'Oh all right.' Hilary allowed Pat to take it. 'But maybe it belongs to someone and we'll have to put it back.'

'What would they have put it up there for?' Mary spoke as they all clustered round Pat. Pat was already unscrewing the lid and lifted out a piece of folded paper. She opened it out.

'Oh!' she stared at it.

'What is it?' The others peered over her shoulder.

'It says, "To The Brownies", it's some kind of message, but I can't read it.'

'Why not?' asked Maureen.

'It's all little drawings, pin men, it's —'

Hilary snatched it from her.

'That's semaphore.'

'Can you read it?' asked Joan.

'No,' Hilary admitted, 'none of us can, but it's in the Brownie Handbook.'

'I know.' Pat reached for the paper again but Hilary held it out of her reach.

'We'll have to get a handbook and work it out.'

'I bet Brown Owl put it there for us to find,' said Valerie solemnly.

'I bet she didn't,' retorted Joan, 'or she'd have given us a clue that it was there.'

Pat had managed to grab the message again.

'Yes, it is semaphore. Let's go and get a handbook at our house and read it.'

'We'll all go then,' decided Hilary.

They ran along the footpath over the field back to the village. Soon they were poring over the semaphore page of the handbook. Hilary called out each letter and Pat wrote them down.

'"HELP", that's the first word.'

Underneath they read.

'SEVEN MANOR SQUARE.'

That was all.

'That's the old people's bungalows, someone at number seven needs help, come on.' Hilary beckoned the others and started towards the door.

'We'll be back soon,' Peggy called to her surprised mother as they all tore down the stairs and out of the front door.

'They're up to something again,' Mrs Martin sighed to herself. 'Now I wonder what it is this time.'

When they had crossed the field again and reached the tree they hesitated at the entrance to the Square.

'There's no numbers on the doors, bother!' exclaimed Joan.

'They probably start from the far side, at the main entrance,' said Hilary.

They ran round the Square until they came to the road entrance, and began to count the completed houses to the left from there. The ones on the right hadn't yet been finished.

'Here it is.'

They stopped at the small front garden.

Suddenly they were silent and stood in a little group, wondering.

Suppose it turned out to be someone frightening. What kind of help could be needed? Maybe it would just turn out to be a silly joke.

'Oh come on.'

Hilary broke the silence.

She marched up to the front door and rang the bell.

Chapter 2

There was a tense silence. From somewhere inside came a muttered exclamation. A moment later the door opened a crack and the grey head of a woman with glasses and a sharp nose peered out.

'Well?'

'We, er, eh, got your message,' stammered Hilary, suddenly nervous.

'Message!' The door opened further to reveal a tall thin figure dressed in dark brown, 'what message?'

'In semaphore,' Hilary sounded braver now. 'In the tree, saying you needed help, it was addressed to the Brownies, and that's us.'

'Semaphore, tree, Brownies.' The voice sounded bewildered. 'I don't know what you mean, but I do need help, yes, I certainly do. How many of you are there?' She stared at the group.

'Seven,' piped up Joan.

'Well, I suppose you might do, come in, don't stand there gaping.'

She stood back and the Brownies filed into the little hall. There was barely enough room for them all.

'Bother,' whispered Maureen to Valerie, 'it's the wrong house.'

The woman closed the door and sighed.

'I don't know whether seven children would be able to do it.' She gazed down at them. From the side view her nose looked like a beak, giving her the appearance of a hawk. Her hair was drawn back in a bun. They stared around in silence.

At the far end of the hall was an open door leading into the sitting-room, and jammed in the entrance was a fireside chair with wooden arms.

'It's stuck, those stupid removal men, I *told* them to put it in the sitting-room, but they left it in the bedroom, I've tried to move it into the sitting-room just now but it's stuck and I just can't get it through!' Her voice sounded weak and tired.

'We can do it.' Hilary elbowed her way to the front of the group and faced them.

'Mary, Peggy and Pat and Val, push, the rest of us will pull, come on!'

She scrambled over the wedged chair into the room beyond, followed by Joan and Maureen. The arms of the chair were tightly jammed against the doorposts. They pushed and pulled and panted while the woman stood wringing her hands and

exclaiming 'Oh dear, oh dear, oh *dear*!' They wiggled and turned and lifted it and suddenly it went through just as those behind gave an extra big push. Hilary, Joan and Maureen fell backwards with the chair on top of them and the others sprawled laughing and shouting on top of it.

'We've done it,' Mary declared proudly as they picked themselves up, 'haven't we?'

'Thank you, yes, er yes,' the woman pulled the chair upright. The only damage was to the paint on the doorposts. 'I'll have to reward you all of course.'

'Oh, er, no thanks,' Hilary quickly replied.

'Brownies don't take rewards for doing good turns, anyway, it was fun!'

'Fun!' sniffed the woman, 'fun! Moving isn't fun I can tell you, nothing but worry, worry, and all that traipsing in and out, in and out, wearing out the carpet, packing and unpacking!' She sat down on the chair looking tired.

In the corner of the room was a big packing case. Some of the contents had already been placed on the shelves of the cupboard at one end of the room, and crumpled newspaper littered the floor. Joan flew around picking up the pieces of paper.

'We *could* help you unpack.' In her tidy mind she longed to see the shelves neatly stacked, and besides, it would be interesting to see what sort of china lay underneath all that packing stuff. It looked rather like a lucky dip at the school fete, you never knew what you might get until it was unwrapped.

'We've got to go to number seven,' Hilary scowled at her. 'We've got to help there, like the message said.' Surely Joan couldn't have forgotten? And now they were wasting time.

'Where is number seven please?'

'Next door, I suppose,' said the woman, 'this is number six but they haven't put the numbers on the doors yet, like a lot of other things they haven't done, windows not painted, footpath not made up,' she grumbled.

'Who lives next door?' asked Valerie.

'Oh I wouldn't know, I don't believe in making free with the neighbours, it isn't a good thing at all, one should keep oneself to oneself.'

'That's what my nan said,' Mary agreed, 'she said they'd always be on the doorstep and she didn't want that, she said —'

Things weren't going at all as Hilary had planned. She glared at Mary and interrupted.

'We've got to go to Number seven.' She waved the semaphore message.

'Let me see,' ordered the woman. She stared at the paper.

'It's semaphore,' Maureen explained patiently, 'for sending messages, specially if there's an emergency.'

'Ridiculous! Little girls of your age! You should be playing with dolls.'

'Oh we do,' Maureen assured her, 'we like dolls but we do other things as well, at Brownies, like —'

'Can we go now please?' Hilary was edging towards the hall.

'If you like we'll come back another time and help you again.' Joan felt sorry for the old lady.

'My name is Miss McNab, and you can come back again if you wish but I don't need you all, two will do. I couldn't stand more than two at a time, but two could help, yes.' Her face creased into a thousand lines as she frowned and rubbed her forehead. Her glasses had slipped further down her beaky nose revealing large grey eyes.

As the door closed behind them they gave sighs of relief. They stared at the door of number seven. There wasn't a sign of anybody. There were no net curtains at the window and they could see flowers on a table in the room so someone must have moved in. Before they had time to think about it Hilary rang the bell. There was no answer. Just as she was about to ring again there was a shuffling noise inside and the door opened very slowly.

Chapter 3

The face that looked out was quite the opposite to Miss McNab's. It had brown eyes that lit up as it smiled and creased the rosy cheeks. It belonged to a very small woman wearing a gay flowered apron and a pink blouse. Hilary felt immediately that it must be the right house.

'We've come,' she said, 'the Brownies.'

The mouth grew into the jolliest smile as the head turned slightly on one side and gazed at the little group clustering behind Hilary. She looked like a bird too, but a cheerful, friendly robin, not a hawk.

'I knew it, so my idea did work after all.' She threw the hall door wide open.

'Welcome Brownies, come in.'

They found themselves in a bright sitting-room with flowers in a copper jug on the mantelpiece and on the table, and pictures on the walls.

'We went next door by mistake,' Valerie told her, feeling quite at home already, 'but I'm glad

we did because her chair was stuck and we fixed it.'

'She hasn't got tidy yet, she's only just moved in,' added Joan.

'So my neighbour is still in a mess, poor thing, I know what that's like,' said their friend. 'I've only just got sorted out myself and it wasn't easy.'

The Brownies noticed she was leaning on a stick and her fingers were quite twisted and swollen.

'I've got arthritis in my hands, as you can see, and in my hip too, but I can still get around and do things for myself, so I'm lucky.' She smiled again cheerfully as if these things didn't matter at all. 'Sit down on the floor now like you do at Brownies so that we can talk.'

Though she was small and fragile looking her voice sounded as if she was used to being obeyed. They sat in a small semi circle and their friend sat in a wing chair facing them.

'My name is Mrs Taylor. I've got some explaining to do, so I'd better speak first. I know you're wondering what that message was all about. You *did* find it I suppose, otherwise you wouldn't be here?'

'*I* found it, I saw it when I was standing on my head looking up at the tree,' said Pat proudly.

'Some of my Brownies used to do headstands,' said Mrs Taylor, 'I was a Brownie Guider for many years in the past, before I became too old and stiff. I haven't been here very long,' she went on, 'and don't know anyone yet, so I was a bit lonely and my neighbour isn't very friendly.'

'She told us she likes to keep herself to herself,' agreed Hilary.

Mrs Taylor nodded.

'I know. Anyway one day I saw some of you walking along the Square in your uniforms and another day standing under that tree, and thought of a possible way to get to know you that would be fun. I knew that if you came that way there was a chance you might see a message in the tree, if you were really wide awake. Of course I was hoping you'd be signallers, able to read semaphore that is, as I do need some help.'

'We don't really know semaphore,' Maureen admitted, 'but we looked at the handbook and made it out.'

'Good, that's a start. It's like a secret language, and the better you know it the more fun you can have with it. Of course, you never know, it could be useful in an emergency too. Now I do need help with shopping, and I thought if I could write some of the items on a shopping list in semaphore, and you could decipher it, the better you'd get at signalling. Of course, I'd have to be sure you got the right message, I couldn't have you buying half a kilo of sausages when I really wanted half a kilo of semolina!'

'Can I do it please?' begged Hilary.

'I'd like to too,' said Peggy and Pat together. There was a chorus of voices all clamouring to help.

'We'll have two at a time and then you can all learn it,' said Mrs Taylor.

'I'll try for Signaller Badge,' cried Hilary

excitedly, 'there is one, I saw it in the book, and there are flags in the cupboard in the hut.'

'You must tell your Brown Owl and see if she is agreeable to your visiting me,' said Mrs Taylor, 'and if so you can arrange who is to come first. I'm sure she'll be pleased about Signaller Badge, it could be very useful.'

Mary had been gazing around the sitting-room when she suddenly saw, on a shelf in a glass fronted cabinet in the corner of the room, a beautiful doll with pink cheeks, blue eyes, and a long dress. Mrs Taylor saw her staring at it.

'You've noticed the doll?'

She went to the cabinet and took it out. They crowded around her with delighted exclamations.

'Isn't she beautiful? She was given to me when I was a little girl,' said Mrs Taylor. 'Her name is Emma, she was made about 1910 or 1912.'

The doll had a tight waisted dress of pink brocade, a high neck and big wide sleeves. A row of tiny buttons trimmed the front of the bodice, and her golden hair was piled on the top of her head. Mrs Taylor said it was Edwardian and quite valuable. Emma had to be handled very carefully but everyone was able to have a close look. They had never seen a doll like her before.

'I love dolls,' sighed Maureen, 'I've got six.'

'So do I,' echoed Mary. 'Last Christmas Mum gave me a baby doll, that's Sarah, and I've got Peter and Christina and Victoria and John,' she counted on her fingers, 'that's five, Oh, and lots of animals, there's —'

'Miss McNab next door said semaphore is ridiculous and we should be playing with dolls,' interrupted Hilary. 'We do like dolls, but I don't see why we can't do both.'

'Of course you can,' agreed Mrs Taylor, 'and lots of other things too.'

'That's what I told her,' said Maureen, 'but she didn't listen.'

'I expect she's upset with the moving in.' Mrs Taylor put the doll back in the cabinet and closed the door, 'and she's living in the past when little girls were only expected to play with dolls.'

Before going home Mrs Taylor gave them squash and biscuits and said it didn't matter at all about crumbs on the carpet. She didn't say anything when Valerie ate faster than any of the others and finished off the last two biscuits on the plate, though they were sure she noticed, her sharp brown eyes looked as if they wouldn't miss anything.

On the way home they stopped under the tree once more.

'I've got it,' announced Hilary, swinging off the lower branch.

'Got what?' asked Joan.

'The Venture, silly. We can help the old people in Manor Square, others besides Miss McNab and Mrs Taylor, they'd probably all like help.'

She was thinking of Signaller Badge too. It was a kind of Venture that might lead on to something more exciting. Of course none of them could know just then how true that would turn out to be!

Chapter 4

When Brown Owl heard about Mrs Taylor and the semaphore message she thought the suggested Venture a great idea.

'I've been thinking about the residents in Manor Square,' she said, 'and meaning to visit them for some time, as they live so near the Manor, where the stables used to be. I'll go tomorrow and see if some of them would like Brownies to lend a hand. I'll be very interested to meet Mrs Taylor, especially as she's been a Guider.'

'I'll visit any of the others for the Venture but I don't want to go to Miss McNab,' said Mary, 'she's horrid.'

'She's probably only horrid because she's in a muddle and doesn't want to be friendly with anyone,' said Peggy.

'I'd like to go again,' offered Joan. 'I didn't think she was really horrible, she could be quite nice underneath.'

Brown Owl said nobody was to visit until she

had called on the other residents too to see if they would like help from the Pack.

Maureen, Joan and Hilary all wanted to work for Signaller Badge. They got out the flags and had a lesson later in the meeting.

The following week Brown Owl told them the Venture could start. She had specially chosen Joan and Valerie to visit Miss McNab on Saturday. She said she knew they would be sensible and not do anything to upset the old lady who seemed quite glad for them to come. Hilary and Maureen were to be first to visit Mrs Taylor for the semaphore shopping, as they were working for the badge. Peggy and Pat were to go to Mr Jones who lived on the far side of the Square at number 21, and who needed gardening help, while Mary would go with another Brownie to Mrs Hamilton at number 17. They would all be able to take turns in visiting Mrs Taylor and reading her semaphore shopping list.

'Of course there must be rules,' said Miss McNab when Valerie and Joan went to her house the following week. They were in the sitting-room once more where the packing case had vanished and items were stacked on the table and on top of the cupboard. 'The first rule is *no chattering*, I can't bear noise, it gives me a head-ache. Second rule, Do what you're told.' She wagged her finger and nodded her head and her glasses slipped down her nose. 'Now do you understand? I've told Miss Atkins, your, er, leader, I've forgotten that queer name you call her.'

'Brown Owl,' said Valerie.

'Yes, Brown Owl, I've told her I'll accept her offer of children's help and see how we get on, but only on condition she sent me two quiet, sensible ones.'

'We are sensible,' said Joan.

'I only hope so,' Miss McNab seemed jumpy and nervous. She pushed her glasses further back on her nose and pointed to the things on the table. 'Now all those cups and saucers and plates have to go in that cupboard, the cups on the hooks inside, the knives and forks in the cutlery drawer, it's on the top left.'

'Yes, Miss McNab, can I start now? I'll be ever so careful.'

Valerie was to use the carpet sweeper on the hall carpet and then sweep the kitchen floor. Soon the only sound was the squeak of the carpet sweeper and the tinkle of knives and forks as Joan sorted them out.

'Mrs Taylor lives next door, she is number seven and it was the right house,' Joan remarked after a little while, 'and she has a lovely doll. It's very old, it's in her cabinet with glass doors, it has a pink dress with buttons on it.'

'Is that so?' Miss McNab who was dusting the bookcase and whose back was turned to Joan looked round sharply, dropping the duster as she did so, for a moment she almost smiled. Then she stooped to pick up the duster. 'I never gossip about neighbours.'

'I like dolls,' went on Joan, 'but I don't play with them all the time, I —'

'That will do,' said Miss McNab sternly, 'no chattering.'

'Oh I forgot,' Joan clapped a hand over her mouth and silence reigned once more.

Next door, Hilary and Maureen had arrived for the shopping. Mrs Taylor handed them a short list, the last two items of which were:

They had brought the handbook and soon read the words as

Half kilo tomatoes
Six eggs.

'We're going over to the Manor this afternoon. Brown Owl is going to help us to send semaphore words from the balcony at the back,' Hilary told her, 'Maureen and Joan and me, we've been practising every day, but we can't do sentences yet.'

Mrs Taylor looked pleased.

'Your Brown Owl was so nice when she called, she told me your names, but it's going to be a little while before I get to know you all.'

'In a way, it's a kind of signalling Venture,' said Hilary as they skipped past the tree and along the footpath across the field, swinging the shopping basket, 'because we might be able to get Signaller's Badge while we're helping in the Square.'

'But that won't be for ages, we don't know all the alphabet yet. Colonel Atkins is going to test us, Brown Owl said so, so we'll have to work terribly hard,' said Maureen. Knowing how particular he was, he'd be sure to expect a high standard.

Brown Owl was ready when the three of them went to the Manor later that day, carrying the flags. They had each decided on a word to send, but only Brown Owl knew what that word was. At the back of the Manor was a long garden with a high wall around it. But it was dotted with fruit trees and shrubs so it wasn't easy to see someone at the other end, specially if they were sending messages. She pointed to a little balcony on the second floor.

'The signaller can stand up there, the other two stand out of earshot with me at the end of the garden, then the next signaller can go up.'

The Manor was a very old house. It had wooden panelling in the square hall, winding passages and solid oak doors that were heavy to push open. It was the sort of house that was exciting to explore, that might contain secrets of the past that no one knew about.

Brown Owl led the way up the wide staircase, along a passage, and opened a door. It was a big room with a fireplace and an alcove at each side of it. The room was quite bare because it was soon to be re-decorated, and the wallpaper was peeling from the walls in places. A glass door led out to the balcony. Brown Owl opened it and went outside.

'There's plenty of room out here to stand and signal, but be careful of the floorboards by the fireplace.' She came back into the room and placed her foot gently on a squeaky board. 'Some of them are a bit loose and will have to be repaired soon.

Joan can be first to signal. Are you ready?'

Joan stood outside holding the flags while Brown Owl and the other two went out into the garden again. She could see them walking down the flagged path between the flowerbeds. They turned and waved and stood looking up at her. She began to signal.

Hilary and Maureen both read the word KELPIE correctly. Joan left the balcony and re-appeared in the garden. Now it was Hilary's turn, while Maureen and Joan read the word VENTURE.

When it came to Maureen's turn she ran into the house and stood still for a moment, alone in the hall, listening. The Colonel was in his study and everything was very quiet. The only sound came from the steady ticking of the old grandfather clock in the corner, with brass figures and painted flowers on the face. A stair creaked as she stepped on it and hurried up to the landing above. She pushed open the door of the room and went in.

Hilary had left the flags propped up against the wall next to the fireplace. Forgetting Brown Owl's warning she reached for the flags and must have stepped on a loose board, for all of a sudden one end gave under her weight, while the other rose up like a see-saw and her foot disappeared below!

'Ow!' she clutched at the wall for support.

Carefully she withdrew her foot and stared at the gaping hole. Then she dropped to her knees and peered in. There was something down there! It was dark inside and not very inviting but she could just see the outline of something that looked a bit like —' With fast beating heart she put in her hand and grasped the object. She drew it out with a gasp of amazement!

Chapter 5

'What's keeping Maureen?' Brown Owl looked anxiously up at the balcony.

'It's ages since she went in,' Joan was hopping up and down in impatience.

'Shall I go and see?' Hilary was just about to set off when Brown Owl called her back.

'No, here she is.'

Maureen appeared on the balcony and waved the flags up and down to show she was about to start. Then she signalled the letters C and O. She put the flags down and looked at the handbook.

'Now she's forgotten the next letter,' said Hilary in disgust.

'Here it comes, watch her,' directed Brown Owl.

'M, E, "Come",' said Hilary and Joan together.

'That's not the word she told me she was going to send,' said Brown Owl.

Maureen had put the flags down and was beckoning urgently.

'Come on, something's up.' Hilary started down the garden path, followed by Joan and Brown Owl.

They found Maureen kneeling by the fireplace. 'Look what I found!'

She was holding a doll. 'It must have been down there for years and years, it's all dirty. A board broke and my foot went in.' She was pointing to the hole.

'Be careful, there may be other loose ones,' warned Brown Owl.

She took the doll from Maureen's outstretched hand. It had once been beautiful, anyone could see that. It was a very elegant lady doll with china head, blue eyes and the remains of golden hair. A full length tattered dress clung to the body. It looked as if the mice had been at work and some of the sawdust stuffing was coming out. It had one tiny green earring, the other was missing.

'Whew! I wonder how long it's been down there? I'll get a torch and see if there's anything else.' Brown Owl handed the doll back to Maureen and went in search of a torch.

'Did you *see* anything else?' breathed Joan, taking a careful step nearer the hole and staring down.

'No, but I saw the doll. I put my hand in,' replied Maureen.

'Ugh, it's probably all spidery!' shivered Joan, '*I* wouldn't put my hand down there.'

'I didn't see any spiders, but there probably were some,' Maureen said carelessly as if spiders meant nothing to her, though privately she wasn't very fond of them either.

Brown Owl came back with a torch and flashed it into the hole.

'Can't see anything else.'

'It's a bit like Mrs Taylor's doll,' said Hilary, 'it's got the same sort of dress, or *had*.'

The floorboard squeaked and creaked as Brown Owl pushed it back in place. Some of the old wood had splintered. They found a duster and dusted the doll's face and hair and dress.

'I'm sure it could be repaired, she was such a lovely doll once,' said Brown Owl.

She agreed they could take the doll to Mrs Taylor on Saturday to show her, and see if she could guess its age.

'By Jove!' barked the Colonel when they took it into the study where he was working at his desk, 'a doll! That's interesting, very interesting indeed. Never know what you'd find in these old houses. Have to get that floor repaired before the decorators come. Dangerous. Can't have people falling into holes.'

He examined the doll closely.

'Get it repaired, find out its history, where it came from. Must have belonged to some child, sometime. Find out!' It sounded like an order.

'I'm sure it didn't belong to the last owners of the Manor,' said Brown Owl. 'It's older than that, but I'll write and ask them.'

She promised to patch it up when she got time, and make it a new dress, but at present she was too busy.

They were to call for the doll on Saturday on their way to Manor Square to visit Mrs Taylor.

'I wonder what its name was?' said Joan thoughtfully.

'She, not it,' corrected Maureen, for whom the doll was already beginning to be a real person, 'and if she was mended and had a new dress she could look just as nice as Mrs Taylor's Emma.'

They were looking forward to showing the doll to her but when the three of them got to number seven Manor Square on Saturday they were in for a disappointment. There was no answer to their knock.

'She can't have gone out, she knew we were coming.' Hilary peered through the sitting-room window, but there wasn't a sign of anyone.

Maureen knocked again.

Joan suddenly had a dreadful thought.

'Maybe she's fallen down inside and can't get to the door.'

She opened the letter-box and called through it.

'Mrs Taylor, are you all right?'

There was no answering groan, not a sound.

As she released the letter-box she glanced down and tensed.

'Look!'

On the ground just in front of the doorstep was a large arrow made from three sticks, the kind used to support plants in the garden. It definitely was an arrow, although Joan's foot had already knocked a bit of it sideways. It was pointing to the left of the hall door, towards the little shed which all the houses had.

'There might be something here.' Hilary examined the door which was closed with a small bolt.

At that moment she saw another arrow, drawn in white chalk on a large stone, pointing to the door of the shed.

She pulled back the bolt and the door swung open. As the daylight flooded in they saw a white

envelope lying on top of an upturned flowerpot just inside the door. It was labelled BROWNIES. Hilary was first to snatch it up. She tore it open, and read the message aloud.

'I'm sorry I have had to go away for a little while, but I hope you will go on practising semaphore. In the meantime, do you think you could help all the residents of Manor Square by making a map showing us how to get to such places as the post office, library, chemist's shop, public telephone? It would be very useful. Thank you very much. I will look forward to seeing you when I return.'

S. Taylor.

'Oh bother!' cried Joan, 'and she doesn't say when she'll be back, it mightn't be for ages.'

'I'd like to make a map,' said Hilary slowly. 'I could do it for part of my Highway badge.'

'Here's Valerie,' said Joan.

Valerie had come to keep their appointment with Miss McNab next door. Hilary stuffed the note into her pocket.

'Don't tell her about making the map, she'd want to do it too, and we can't *all* do it.'

'Show her the doll,' ordered Joan.

They opened the paper in which it was wrapped. It was filled with sawdust!

'The poor thing, she's bleeding!' exclaimed Maureen. Joan told Valerie the story of the find while Maureen tied her clean hanky round the doll's leg.

'Come on, Miss McNab will be waiting for us.' Joan grabbed Valerie's arm and led her to the garden gate. 'And remember don't talk, she doesn't like noise.'

They wished they could take the doll to show her, but sawdust spilled on the carpet would only make her cross. They decided not to say anything at all about what had happened at the Manor, it would be much safer not to.

'We need more sawdust, her leg has gone flat,' complained Hilary, 'but where can we get any?'

'Sawdust.' Maureen gave a skip of excitement causing more of it to trickle out of the paper wrapping on to the ground at her feet. 'I know where we can get sawdust.'

Chapter 6

'Where?' asked Hilary.

'Mr Holmes, he has plenty.'

Hilary wished she had thought of it first.

'Yes, it's ages since we went there, let's go now.'

Mr Holmes was their carpenter friend who had his workshop in Manor Square in what had once been the old coach house, where some of the Brownies used to meet in secret not so long ago. But he still lived in the quaint old cottage in Church Lane.

As they drew near they could hear the sound of a carpenter's plane. The workshop door was open, and there he was, shirt sleeves rolled up, and wearing a brown apron. His bushy eyebrows were drawn together in a frown of concentration. Sawdust and wood shavings lay thick on the floor.

They stood silently watching for a few moments before he showed that he had seen them. Then he straightened his back, readjusted his glasses and smiled.

'Well, what's news?'

For answer Maureen unwrapped the parcel and held its contents out for him to see.

'Can you give us some sawdust please, her leg is damaged.'

'Sawdust! plenty of that, help yourselves.' He wiped his hands on the apron and took the doll. 'Where did you get this?'

They took it in turns to tell him the story.

'Quite a find! Ancient isn't it, and worth repairing. I think she'll need a new leg.'

They scooped sawdust from the floor and filled a small bag he gave them. He told them to put more sawdust into the leg and bandage it, until a new leg was made.

'Look at the note Mrs Taylor left for us.' Hilary showed it to him.

Mr Holmes read it over twice before folding it up and handing it back, looking thoughtful.

'Very useful a map would be, to those residents new to Ferndale. Of course I've lived here for many years so I'd know my way round blindfold. Mind you, there are a few other places you could include that the old folks round here might like to know about.'

'What sort of places?' asked Maureen.

'Well,' Mr Holmes spoke slowly, hands on hips, as he gazed out through the open door. 'You could tell them where the best blackberry bushes are to be found, they're not far from here, in the footpath field you know. And do you know where they could find wild mushrooms in August or September? I do. They're delicious fried for breakfast. And you could put in the new seat that's just been put near the bus stop in Market Street.'

'I know where the mushrooms grow,' said Hilary eagerly, 'we picked some in the buttercup field last year.' She was beginning to think the map making could be really interesting.

'Thank you for the sawdust,' said Maureen as they turned to go.

'Any time, always plenty here, I work so hard you see,' smiled Mr Holmes. He waved goodbye and bent over his work again.

Maureen went home with Hilary and as they entered by the back door they heard voices in the living-room.

'I bet that's the vicar, Mr Sinclair,' whispered Hilary, 'Mum said he was going to call soon.'

Maureen hung back, but Hilary pulled her arm.

'Come on, we'll show him the doll, he won't bite, don't be shy!'

'I'm not,' Maureen retorted hotly. It was only that she didn't like starting a conversation with a grown up she didn't know, and the vicar was new. He was sitting on the sofa stroking Hilary's black cat, Sooty, who had climbed on to his lap, purring loudly. Sooty jumped to the floor and wound himself around Hilary's legs as soon as they entered the room.

'Yes, I believe the Manor is very old,' Mr Sinclair was saying to Hilary's mother, Mrs Anderson, 'Colonel Atkins asked me to call there so —'

He broke off and smiled at the two girls.

'We found this in the Manor, hidden under the floor, and it's very old too.' Hilary unwrapped the parcel to show him.

'*I* found it,' corrected Maureen, 'we were all doing semaphore from the balcony and when it was my turn my foot went down a hole in that room and I found the doll underneath.' She liked Mr Sinclair on sight and knew immediately he would be interested.

'Well, what a find!' he exclaimed, 'but she's injured!'

'The mice,' explained Hilary, 'she'll have to have a new leg, the stuffing has come out.'

Mrs Anderson sent Hilary to the first aid box in the bathroom to get a roll of bandage. While they were talking to Mr Sinclair she packed some sawdust from the bag they had brought into the leg and bandaged it tightly.

'That should do for the present until it's

repaired. I wonder who owned it and what her name was?'

'I wish we could find out,' said Maureen, 'but it was years and years ago, maybe about seventy years. It looks like Mrs Taylor's and hers is about that age.'

Mr Sinclair stood up and went to the window.

'I wonder if there are any records in the church that might help?'

'Records?' Hilary looked puzzled.

'The parish records of births, marriages and deaths,' he explained. 'If we could find who owned the Manor about 1910, then the likely owner could have been a little girl of that family, that's if the doll is about the age you think it might be. I find these old records very interesting myself.' He put down his cup of tea, looking thoughtful. He was a tall, thin, serious looking man. Clever, people said he was, always reading.

'Like to call in to the church with me on my way home and we'll have a look?'

Not long afterwards they were poring over the huge dusty volumes in the vestry, as the vicar turned the pages.

'In 1906 a girl was born to the owners of the Manor at that time. 12th April, 1906,' he read. 'Charlotte Anne, daughter of Emily and Percy Adams. By 1910 she would have been four years old, and by the time she was eight or nine she could have been playing with a doll made about 1910. Then, there was a boy born in 1908. James Percy.'

Mr Sinclair turned the pages of another huge book, while Hilary and Maureen stood on tiptoe to stare at the faded writing.

'I see that in 1913, Emily Adams, their mother, died, and the following year their father also died, probably killed in the first war. There's a memorial tablet to the Adams family in the church.'

'Poor Charlotte Anne,' said Hilary. 'She put the doll in a secret hiding place under the floor, and

when her parents died she was taken to live with someone else and forgot and left it behind, and when she remembered, it was too late.'

'That's one explanation,' agreed the Vicar. 'If it did belong to her. Of course there were several different owners of the Manor after that. Interesting old house,' he mused, slowly closing the books. 'Interesting, could hold a few secrets.'

'Let's call her Charlotte Anne,' suggested Hilary. Maureen agreed it was a nice, easy to say, sort of name, and seemed to suit the doll.

Their footsteps echoed on the bare stone floor

of the church as they left the vestry and walked down past the rows of empty pews. Sunlight, slanting through the stained glass windows lit up a marble memorial tablet on the wall in memory of Charlotte Anne's parents. The three of them stood for a moment staring up at it in silence.

'I know we'll find out sometime who she belonged to,' Maureen declared, 'I just know we will.'

Hilary didn't answer, she wasn't so sure.

'Maybe you will,' said the vicar softly. 'Stranger things have happened, stranger things have happened!'

Chapter 7

The Brownies all agreed that 'Charlotte Anne' was a good name for the doll. Brown Owl took her to Pack Meeting the following week to show them, and Maureen related the story of what happened at the semaphore practice. She made it sound as exciting as possible. In her mind she was already beginning to work out a story about a hidden doll for her Writer Badge, and was going to start on it straight away.

Hilary was going to start on making that map too. She had already put Manor Square on a large piece of stiff paper and drawn in the tree at the footpath field entrance.

One afternoon Maureen and Joan went with her to the Square to see where to put the other places. Peggy and Pat caught up with them as they entered the Square from the field side.

'Mr Jones has bought a budgie,' Peggy told them, 'it's yellow and green and he's going to call it Cheeky, because it is.'

'And we're going to clean the cage out and give it fresh water when we come,' said Pat.

'That has to be done every day though,' added Peggy, 'but Mr Jones will let us do it on Saturdays.'

'Does it talk?' asked Hilary.

'Not yet, but it could, if we teach it,' Peggy stopped at number 21 and knocked.

'I wish Miss McNab had a budgie,' sighed Joan, 'but I don't think she'd like one, she'd think it was too messy, they sometimes drop seed on the floor.'

'I'm glad we're not visiting her,' retorted Hilary. 'Mrs Taylor is much nicer and she's fun too.'

'But now she's gone away and you haven't anyone,' Joan reminded her, 'and anyway I like Miss McNab and so does Val. She told us last time that she looks forward to our coming.'

'Humph!' snorted Hilary. It was disappointing that Mrs Taylor had gone away just as they were getting to know her, but just now the most important thing was to get the map finished by the time she returned. She opened it up and put a mark where the road entrance was to go, and another where the footpath led across the field.

'What else are you going to put in?' asked Joan, 'besides the church and library and everything?'

'We'll go and see where exactly the blackberry bushes are,' Hilary decided, 'so that in the autumn they can pick them and make blackberry jam.'

In the footpath field they crossed to the side which bordered the backs of the houses in the Square, and soon saw the pinkish white flowers of the blackberry bushes that would be full of berries later on.

'M-mm, wish there were some to eat now,' sighed Joan, 'look, there are a whole lot more bushes behind this one.' She pushed aside the prickly stems, and bent down, peering straight ahead.

'What's up?' demanded Hilary.

Joan didn't reply immediately.

She knelt down, holding a thorny branch away from her face.

'There's a big sort of stone in there, lying on its side, I can see writing on it.'

'Where?' Hilary and Maureen knelt beside her.

'There.'

They looked where her finger pointed. Suddenly the bramble escaped from Joan's hand and snapped back, hitting Hilary's head and entangling her long, red hair.

'Ow! silly, now I'm caught,' she shrieked.

'Hold on.' Joan managed to pull the prickly stem free.

'Maybe it's a tombstone and a pet animal was buried there years ago,' suggested Maureen.

'It's not,' replied Joan. 'I saw the writing on it and it said something about "the bright hours".'

'Then it's probably a sundial,' said Hilary, 'you can tell the time by it, but only when the sun is shining. They used to be in gardens.'

'What used to be?' asked a voice behind them.

They turned to find Peggy and Pat again.

'Sundials, and there might be one in there, so it could have been a garden, once,' said Maureen.

Peggy and Pat immediately lay flat on their tummies, one behind the other, and began to crawl between the bushes. But it was no good, they were pricked and stung. Pat backed out, still on hands and knees, followed by Peggy, who danced up and down holding her left hand.

'I'm stung, there are nettles in there!'

'Quick, a dock leaf.' Joan had noted a clump of them growing nearby. Peggy held out her hand while Joan rubbed it hard with the crumpled leaf. Soon the pain eased.

'Oh don't let's bother trying to get in, it doesn't matter what's in there,' said Peggy.

'Yes, it does matter,' retorted Hilary. 'I want to find out anyway. We can't crawl in but I've just thought of something.'

'What?' asked Peggy.

They all stared at Hilary expectantly.

Not far behind the blackberry bushes rose a tall, thick hedge, and above it could be seen the roofs of the houses in Manor Square.

Hilary pointed to the hedge.

'If we go back to the Square there might be a way of getting in by the side of one of the houses, through that hedge.'

'But which house?' asked Maureen.

Hilary counted the roofs starting from the entrance in the field.

'The sixth or seventh would be the nearest to here, let's go and see.'

They went into the Square again and walked quietly along the little alleyway beside the seventh house. This brought them to a rough stony track which led between the tall hedge and the backyards of the houses.

Soon Hilary, who was leading the way, halted. 'Look!'

There was a hole in the hedge, low down. Not a very big hole, but big enough to crawl through.

'I'll go first.'

She knelt on all fours and began to crawl. When there was only one foot to be seen she stopped and the others heard her call out 'Oh!'

'What is it? What's there?' clamoured Peggy and Pat. There was no reply but the foot disappeared and the hedge moved as she stood up on the other side.

Without waiting to be asked Peggy crawled through and Pat followed fast on her sister's heels. The others could hear the three of them talking, and quickly scrambled through the hole which had grown larger already.

They found themselves in a clearing. It was a long, narrow strip of ground between the tall hedge behind them and the thick row of bramble bushes bordering the field in front. There was the fallen sundial not far away and around it grew a carpet of nettles. But between the nettles they could see the remains of flowerbeds bordered with pinks. There was a rosemary bush with tiny blue flowers showing on the tall stems, and a clump of lavender. A faint perfume hung on the air, and for a moment the Brownies stood quite still, breathing it in.

Beside the lavender bush grew another plant

with no flower showing but thick, soft leaves. Peggy pressed a leaf and smelled her fingers.

'M-mm, that's sage, we have it at home, it's a herb, and smells gorgeous.' After that they walked around pressing and smelling the leaves of all the plants they could find.

'It's a herb garden,' said Hilary.

'It *was* one you mean,' corrected Joan. 'It's nothing but a bit of old waste ground now.'

'No it isn't, it's still a garden, even if nobody has bothered about it for years and years,' said Pat.

'It must belong to the Manor,' Hilary said, sniffing a sprig of rosemary, 'but I bet Brown Owl and Colonel Atkins think it's just empty ground. And if it was a herb garden behind the stables years ago there should be an opening into the Manor grounds somewhere.'

One end of the narrow garden was enclosed by the hedge, and as they walked in the opposite direction suddenly they heard the sound of a lawn mower.

'We're in the Manor garden all right,' said Maureen in a half whisper, as if to talk loudly might spoil the peace and quietness she could feel in the air. Somehow she didn't want to find the way out, not just yet.

But they had found it. At least they had found what could be a way out. There was a gap in the hedge ahead, but the two shrubs growing at each side of it had become completely overgrown and almost blocked the entrance. They pushed their way through the tangled mass and found they were in what Colonel Atkins called 'the shrubbery'. It was dark and damp underfoot with rough grass growing between the bushes.

'Come on.' Hilary led the way through it until they reached the lawn bordering the gravel drive leading to the front door of the Manor. The sound of the lawn mower approaching grew louder and louder, and, as they stepped out on to the lawn, Colonel Atkins gave a startled exclamation and stopped short, staring as if he couldn't believe his eyes!

He switched off the motor and for a moment there was silence. Then Peggy giggled and Pat giggled and they all began laughing. Colonel Atkins mopped his brow with a white handkerchief. His shirt sleeves were rolled up and his face was red.

'Playing games in the Manor grounds, eh? Uninvited?' he bellowed.

He was frowning and suddenly they all stopped laughing and looked at Hilary. It was she who had got them here, now she could get them out of it. She could do the explaining and that might not be easy, not when the Colonel was looking annoyed.

Chapter 8

'We weren't exactly playing games and we didn't mean to come into the Manor garden but we got here from the herb garden and we don't know whether it is part of the Manor garden but it probably is even if you don't know and —' gabbled Hilary, then broke off, staring down the drive. The Colonel was frowning as if he hadn't understood a word she said. There was the sound of a car and as it came into view and drew up by the Manor door they saw that it was Brown Owl, returned from her school job in the nearby town of Bayhurst.

They rushed across the lawn in one group and surrounded her as she stepped from the car.

Everyone started talking at once so that she raised her arm for silence, just as if they were at Pack meeting. Colonel Atkins had left the lawn mower and marched across the grass, where he stopped just behind them, with hands on hips.

'Can we show you something we don't think

you know is there?' Hilary asked.

'Where?' asked Brown Owl, looking bewildered.

Hilary took her arm and pulled her towards the lawn in the direction of the shrubbery.

'It's a garden, a herb garden, and it's got a sundial and, lavender, and, er nettles.' Peggy got the chance to explain as they all wended their way through the shrubbery. Hilary held back the trailing undergrowth at the entrance in the hedge, while Brown Owl and her father made their way through.

'By Jove!' The Colonel's favourite exclamation rose above the chatter of voices as they stood and stared around. 'I said this house and grounds could hold a few secrets and now the Brownies seem to have revealed another of them!'

Stepping over the nettles they began to find more herbs. There was a thyme plant, with pinkish purple flowers, some mint, and a tall, feathery sort of grass that Brown Owl said was called fennel.

'It's been unattended for several years, needs a good clean up, all dug over and the hedge clipped,' decided the Colonel. Then he saw the fallen sundial. 'Nice bit of stone. Have to get that repaired. A man I know will do it for me. Get him as soon as possible.'

'The old people in the Square could come here

when it's all tidy again, if you'd allow them,' suggested Hilary, looking up at Colonel Atkins, 'as it's so near their houses, only there would have to be a proper opening in the hedge.'

The Colonel pulled his moustache and looked pleased.

'Now that's an excellent idea, quite excellent. We have enough ground ourselves to keep up, and some of them who can might later on help with it by doing a spot of gardening here themselves. There's a lot to be done first though,' he went on. 'I'd suggest the Brownies might help with the work of clearing it and include that in the Venture my daughter has told me you're doing for the old folk, eh?'

Peggy and Pat were both eager, they liked gardening, and so did Hilary. But Joan and Maureen weren't so keen.

Brown Owl invited them all back to the Manor to talk about it while she made a cup of tea. Hilary spread the map she had brought on the table, and put 'Herb Garden' behind the houses in the Square, for she was quite sure her idea would soon come about. She marked 'Blackberry Bushes' clearly at one side of it, next to the field. Brown Owl said there must have been a fence of some sort there years ago which fell down and the blackberries took over. Another fence could be erected, but she promised the blackberries would remain.

The herb garden might not be ready for a long time yet, Colonel Atkins said, it would depend on how hard they all worked.

Brown Owl told the rest of the Pack about the garden at the next Pack Meeting, and asked for volunteers to help. Mary was one of those who couldn't make up her mind. She liked some kinds of gardening, like planting and watering and watching to see if seeds were coming up, but not weeding and digging. Next time she visited Mrs Hamilton at number 17 she'd crawl through that hedge Hilary had described to have a look at the garden.

Her chance came a few days later.

Mrs Hamilton was out when she knocked at the door, but as it was nearly lunchtime, and the 'Meals on Wheels' van was due, she was sure to return in a minute. Mary sat on the doorstep to wait, and just then she saw the van drive into the Square and a lady got out. She began delivering the little foil-covered dishes to some of the houses. When she reached number 17, Mary told her that Mrs Hamilton wasn't at home.

'Could you take her dinner for her then?' asked the lady, 'that's if you are waiting for her to come back.'

'I'll look after it,' Mary agreed.

She took the two small dishes and put them on her lap. She clasped her hands round them to try to keep in the warmth of the dishes. The moments went by and still Mrs Hamilton didn't come. She could be looking for that hole in the hedge now instead of wasting time waiting here, where there was nothing to do. The opening into the herb garden couldn't be very far away, and it would only take a few minutes.

She put Mrs Hamilton's dinner on the doorstep and ran off down the Square till she found the alleyway leading to the path behind the houses. It didn't take long to find the hole in the hedge. Maybe it wasn't the same one Hilary and the others had found, but it would do, she could just squeeze through. She was glad she was here on her own because now she could do as she liked and didn't have to put up with Hilary's bossiness.

Stepping carefully over the nettles she found the broken sundial and smelled the sage and the lavender that Brown Owl had told them about. She found the remains of a small flowerbed, that would be fun to look after. It wasn't too weedy, and had tiny pink flowers round the edge. She'd ask if she could tidy that one.

The sun had vanished behind clouds and suddenly the garden seemed gloomy, the hedge, tall and forbidding, shutting out the light.

She walked along beside it to find the way out again. But where was it? One or two places looked like holes but weren't big enough to get through. The place she thought she had come through before wasn't a hole at all from this side. Was she shut in? Would she have to stay here for hours and hours? And if she found the way out into the Manor grounds the Colonel might see her and be angry like Hilary had said he was with the others.

With fast beating heart Mary ran up and down, staring at the hedge. Then she dropped to her hands and knees and crawled along, trying all the likely looking places. She was scratched and bruised when at last she found a very thin part of hedge that parted as she pushed her way through. She found she had come out further along the path behind the houses and ran back down it, along one of the alleyways, and into the Square.

Someone was walking ahead of her carrying a shopping bag. When she caught up with the figure she saw that it was Mrs Hamilton.

'What have you been up to?' Mrs Hamilton stared in surprise at Mary's flushed face, and untidy hair. Bits of leaves and grass clung to her dress. Before Mary could reply she went on, 'I've been to Bayhurst for shopping and had to wait half an hour for a bus back. Expect my dinner has arrived, I'm ready for it!'

'It has, it's on the doorstep,' Mary said as they came near number 17.

But then they stopped and gasped. A dog was eating something at the front door. It turned and saw them. Licking its jaws it ran off quickly, leaving a half empty carton of dinner with gravy spilled on the step.

Mrs Hamilton put down the shopping bag and sighed.

'Looks as if I'm not going to have that dinner after all. It's just not my day!'

Chapter 9

Mrs Hamilton picked up the carton and dropped it into the dustbin in her yard. The dog had bitten through the foil lid and torn part of it off. She put the smaller carton, containing her pudding, into the bin too. Although it wasn't open she said she didn't fancy it now that a dog had been sniffing at it.

Mary's face felt hot again as she followed Mrs Hamilton indoors.

'I'll cook a dinner for you,' she said eagerly, 'I've got Cook Badge and I can do potatoes and carrots, and if you've got any sausages I can cook those too.'

'Well now,' Mrs Hamilton lowered her stout figure into a chair and took off her shoes, 'I have some potatoes I was going to cook at the week-end when the dinners don't come, and I believe there are a few sausages in the fridge, have a look lovie.'

Mary found the sausages, two carrots and two potatoes. She washed her hands at the sink and began to prepare the vegetables. When they were boiling she found the frying pan and some fat. Mrs Hamilton tied a big apron round Mary's waist, it came down to her feet, so she tucked it up a bit. Mary was unusually quiet while Mrs Hamilton made herself a cup of tea. Suddenly she burst out.

'It was my fault about your meals-on-wheels dinner. I told the lady I'd keep it until you came but then I put it on the step and went to see the secret herb garden and couldn't find the way out,

and when I did it was too late and —' she stopped because Mrs Hamilton knew the rest.

'Secret herb garden? Where's that?'

To her relief the old lady sounded as if she had forgotten about the loss of the dinner already.

'Some of the others found it when they were in the footpath field looking for blackberry bushes to put on the map, and they found the way in through the hedge behind the houses and —'

By the time Mary stopped for breath the sausages were done. Mrs Hamilton helped her to drain the vegetables and put the sausages on a warm plate, and while Mrs Hamilton was eating Mary kept talking, just allowing time for her to say 'Really!' or 'Fancy that!' or 'Lavender!'

She had just got to the bit about Brown Owl saying that if and when the garden was all put right the residents of the Square might be able to use it, when she heard a shout outside. Rushing to the window she saw Peggy running along the path, with Pat close behind. Peggy was pointing at the roof of one of the houses further down the Square. They disappeared down one of the alleyways between the houses.

'What's happening now?' Mrs Hamilton joined Mary at the window. Since the Brownies had come to brighten up Manor Square life had become much more interesting, she reflected.

'I don't know, can I go and see?'

Mary was already making for the door.

'I'll come back to wash up for you, really I will,' she promised.

'And tell me what they're doing, won't you?' asked the old lady.

Over at number 6, Miss McNab had woken up that morning with a cold. Her nose ran and her head ached. When the two Brownies called she wondered if she should ask them to go away, but if she did she would be all alone and that would be worse. She had grown used to their company now, and they were well behaved. So there they were, sitting at the kitchen table, polishing her spoons and forks and talking to each other in loud whispers, because they knew she didn't like noise. But by the look of them they were polishing themselves too! One had a black smudge on her nose and their hands and arms were covered with polish marks. She just *knew* that when they went to wash their hands they'd put black marks all over her nice clean sink!

'I wish I'd found the herb garden too,' Valerie whispered to Joan as she worked hard on the back of a silver teaspoon. She hadn't even seen the garden yet. She asked Joan if she'd show her where it was, but Joan said she'd better wait until they went with Brown Owl for the gardening.

Miss McNab sat down to read the local newspaper while they were working because she felt tired.

'Dear, oh dear!' they heard her exclaim. 'Dreadful, I don't know what young people are coming to these days!'

'What is it?' Valerie asked, screwing her head round to see the front page of the paper Miss McNab was holding.

'Vandalism again, the telephone box in Market Street has been damaged and that new seat by the bus stop daubed with paint!'

Living alone these days really made one nervous, she thought. You never knew what could happen. She got up and looked out of the window at her little back yard. The small tree overhanging it was in full leaf now.

Suddenly there was a crash. Miss McNab screamed and Valerie and Joan jumped from their seats at the table and rushed to her side.

'There's a vandal now, wrecking the yard!' Her hand flew to her throat and her face paled.

The dustbin had been knocked right over and lay on its side, the contents strewn over the ground. A figure lay sprawled across it and was slowly picking itself up.

'That's not a vandal' cried Valerie, 'it's only Peggy, and she's a Brownie!'

Chapter 10

'I don't care who it is, she's knocked over my dustbin and now look at the mess!'

Miss McNab seemed to have recovered from her fright and was only angry.

Joan and Valerie ran out into the yard to find Peggy, now upright. She had scraped her hands and knees and looked as if she was trying to hold back the tears.

'What are you doing? Miss McNab is furious!' hissed Valerie.

'And look at the bin!' Joan was struggling to right the heavy dustbin while Valerie began to pick up the rubbish.

'I couldn't help it,' snapped Peggy, 'I slipped off the tree when I was chasing the budgie.'

'Budgie!' echoed Joan.

'Mr Jones' Cheeky, it escaped when we were cleaning the cage and flew up there.' She pointed to a branch of the tree overhanging the yard.

'You'd better come in and tell Miss McNab

you're sorry, come on.' Joan grabbed her arm and pushed her through the kitchen into the living-room.

'I'm very sorry,' Peggy began, 'Mr Jones' budgie escaped and was in that tree so I climbed it and the branch bent over and I fell on your dustbin, and it's all our fault the budgie's lost!' Her voice choked as she looked down at her grazed knees.

'Where did it go?' asked Valerie.

'I don't know,' Peggy raised her head, 'I didn't see —' her mouth fell open and she stared at the wall.

There was a sudden silence as they all followed her gaze. There on a shelf was a small green and yellow bird.

'There he is,' cried Peggy. 'Quick, close everything!'

Miss McNab winced as Peggy slammed the doors leading into the kitchen and the hall while Joan rushed to close the window. There was a flutter of wings as Cheeky left his perch on the shelf and landed on the curtain pelmet.

Miss McNab sat down. Things were really quite beyond her control. She blew her nose and closed her eyes. Perhaps when she opened them again everything would have come back to normal. But no, now one of them, the one who had knocked over the dustbin, had dashed out of the room saying she was going to get the bird's cage.

A few yards along the footpath Peggy met Mr Jones carrying the cage. He was a short, stocky man with a cheerful face. Pat, and Mary too, she noticed, were with him, and Mary was asking questions.

'Thought I'd better bring it along just in case we —' he said.

'I've found Cheeky,' cried Peggy joyfully, grabbing his arm. 'This way, he's in Miss McNab's.'

At the hall door they were met by Joan and Valerie with Miss McNab behind them.

'I'm sorry to disturb you Ma'am,' apologised Mr Jones, 'and for the trouble caused, but my budgie disappeared and I've heard he's in your house. Don't think we've met.' He smiled a radiant smile and shook hands with Miss McNab. 'Name's Jones, number 21.'

Mr Jones' warm smile made her feel she would perhaps like to make a friend or two.

They crowded into the living-room. Cheeky was now perching on something on top of the cupboard, a small object with a round top like a miniature travelling trunk.

'Can I stand on a chair?' asked Peggy, dragging a dining chair across the room.

Miss McNab looked at Mr Jones.

'Take your shoes off first,' he ordered, 'and I'll hold the chair.'

When she was standing on it he handed her the cage. The cage door was open and Peggy held it close to the bird.

'Come on Cheeky boy, come into your house,' chorused Peggy and Pat, while Mr Jones whistled encouragingly.

Cheeky seemed to be more interested in examining the object he was perching on, but suddenly he noticed the cage and hopped on to the edge of its open door. A moment later he was inside and looking at himself in the little mirror hanging from the top.

The children cheered as Mr Jones took the cage and closed the door.

'He's safe now. Thanks, Missis, for your assistance.'

'N-not at all,' said Miss McNab faintly, 'her knee's bleeding.' She pointed to Peggy who was getting down from the chair. 'I'll attend to it in the bathroom.'

She pulled a protesting Peggy out of the room, while Mr Jones set off with the cage, followed by Pat and Mary.

Valerie and Joan had finished polishing, and by the time Miss McNab and Peggy re-appeared,

Peggy with a plaster on her knee, they had washed their hands and stacked the spoons and forks away. Peggy looked up to the place where Cheeky had been enticed into the cage.

'What's that thing he was perching on?' she asked curiously.

'It's a doll's travelling trunk, like people had in days past. I had it as a child,' said Miss McNab. 'I was very fond of dolls, and I've kept the trunk all these years. I'll show it to you sometime, but not now, atishoo!' she searched for her hanky, 'it's time you all went home.'

'Miss McNab is quite nice really,' said Peggy when they were outside in the Square again. 'She washed my knee and didn't hurt much, and said I could have been injured when I fell but I wasn't!' She grinned and did a cartwheel just to prove it!

Chapter 11

News soon went round Manor Square that Mrs Taylor was coming back next Wednesday. Mrs Hamilton told Mary, who passed on the information to Hilary when they were working in the herb garden with Brown Owl and the Colonel. Hilary gave a shout of delight and rushed over to tell Brown Owl. Could she and Maureen take Charlotte Anne to show Mrs Taylor on Thursday? she asked. Brown Owl said to give her a day or two to settle in again and then call, and how was the map making going?

'It's just finished,' Hilary told her proudly, 'and I've put in north, south, east and west by reading the compass.'

She was getting on well with the semaphore too. Brown Owl had said she would be ready to be tested next week. Joan and Maureen would have to wait a bit longer but they were to go to the Manor with Hilary for a practice on Friday afternoon.

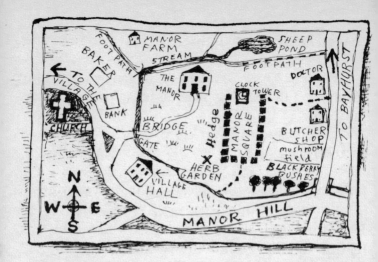

Maureen was beginning to wonder if she'd ever be ready to be tested. She still had to look at the handbook when she was signalling more than one word. When you made a mistake you had to signal the letter E eight times, and that was the letter she now knew better than any in the alphabet!

She dug in the handfork she was using in the herb garden just then and pulled up another few weeds. Would the garden ever look like a real garden again? It was all such hard work! The sundial had been taken away to be repaired, and a lot of the nettles had been dug up, but it still looked overgrown. Colonel Atkins was carting away some of the nettles now in a wheelbarrow. Still, Maureen reflected, if Mrs Taylor was coming home soon it would be fun taking the doll to show her and telling her all that had happened since she went away.

When Hilary, Maureen and Joan went to the Manor on Friday they found the hall full of boxes and bags.

'Jumble for the W.I. jumble sale,' explained Brown Owl. 'Someone will be calling to collect it this afternoon. I'm really glad to be getting rid of it all, we've had a good clear out of everything we don't need.'

There were old clothes, garden tools, pots and pans and some very old broken toys which Brown Owl's young cousins had finished with.

Maureen and Joan waited downstairs while Hilary went up to the balcony to signal to Colonel Atkins in the garden for her badge test. While they were waiting the hall door bell rang. It was a friend of Brown Owl's, another teacher from the school in Bayhurst, Mrs Morris. Brown Owl had told her about the discovery of the doll and she said she would call to see it if she happened to be passing one day.

Brown Owl hurried upstairs to get Charlotte Anne and while she was gone Maureen told the visitor the story of the find. She was becoming better and better at telling it now, and was beginning to learn how to make it sound just as exciting as it really was at the time.

'Very old, how interesting! I think it probably dates from the early 1900's,' exclaimed Mrs Morris as she examined the doll. 'What a pity her leg is damaged.'

'I've promised to repair it as soon as I can,' said Brown Owl.

They walked out to the hall door to say goodbye.

'Lucky find, look after her well, many thanks for letting me see her.' Mrs Morris handed the doll to Maureen and drove off. Just then Hilary came running up to them, smiling happily, followed by the Colonel.

'I've passed, I've passed, hurray!' she held up the semaphore flags with a triumphant flourish.

'Well done,' said Brown Owl. 'Now Joan and I

will go out to the garden and Joan can try to read Maureen's words.'

Maureen laid Charlotte Anne on the hall table and took the flags from Hilary. The others went through the hall and out to the garden and the Colonel went back to his study as Maureen ran up the stairs to the room with the balcony. It had a new floor now and there wasn't a squeak to be heard as she crossed it and took up her position outside. But somehow the letters got mixed up and she signalled 'O' instead of 'P' and 'M' instead of 'N', and each time had to signal 'E' eight times.

Brown Owl sighed.

'She doesn't seem to have improved at all.'

'Can I try now,' begged Joan. She was sure she could do better. She did, but not quite well enough to be tested.

It wasn't fair that Hilary should have passed already thought Maureen grumpily.

'Cheer up,' encouraged Brown Owl as they went into the house again, 'I know you'll both do it in the end if you'll only practise a bit more.'

The Colonel appeared in the hall.

'Jumble's gone, two ladies called and filled up their van while you were outside.'

'Good, now we've got more space,' Brown Owl looked pleased as she glanced around the empty hall.

'Can we take Charlotte Anne now?' asked Hilary. 'We're going to call at Mrs Taylor's tomorrow, and we want to show her.'

'Yes you may.' Brown Owl stood still as if thinking.

'She's, er, where *is* she? Did you take her upstairs, Maureen, when you went to signal? I know you were holding her.'

Maureen didn't answer immediately. She was staring at the hall table. At last she spoke.

'No. I remember I laid her down there,' she said, pointing to it. The table was empty.

Brown Owl turned to Colonel Atkins.

'Did you see the doll there, father?'

He shook his head.

'No. I told the two ladies who called to take everything that was here, and they did.'

There was silence as the dreadful truth dawned. Charlotte Anne had been taken away for jumble!

Chapter 12

Maureen burst into tears.

'They thought she was just any old doll, they've taken her with the broken toys,' she sobbed.

Brown Owl put her arm around her and tried to comfort her.

'It was my fault for not taking her upstairs again straight away, but we were all thinking about semaphore just then. Now we've got to think how we can rescue her, if we can.'

'A plan of campaign,' bellowed the Colonel, pacing up and down the hall, pulling his moustache. 'Must get a plan into action immediately. Telephone the Women's Institute,' he suggested, 'get them to search through their jumble. Mind you,' he admitted, 'judging by the amount of stuff I saw they had in their van, that would be no easy job!'

'We can't do that,' said Brown Owl. 'It would take them hours to search all through it. The sale is tomorrow afternoon. I'd go to it myself and try to find the doll but we're going away for the week-end early tomorrow.'

'We'll go and buy her back, we're sure to find her on a toy stall,' said Hilary eagerly.

'You'd have to be there early,' said Brown Owl. 'This is the biggest jumble sale of the year and there'll be a lot of people there. But, yes, do go with Maureen and do your best. Go straight to the toy section, I'll give you some money.'

It was no wonder that Hilary was the only cheerful Brownie as the three of them went home that evening. Of course she *had* gained Signaller Badge, and she seemed sure the doll would turn up again. But Maureen and Joan were gloomy. Everthing seemed to be going wrong. It was all right for Hilary, and she had the map all ready to show Mrs Taylor when they went there, but it would be no fun telling her about the finding of Charlotte Anne, and then have to tell her the doll had gone.

On the way home they passed the Village Hall. The jumble sale was advertised on a big poster outside.

'Commencing 2 p.m.' it said.

They planned to meet outside at 1.45 p.m. next day. Then they would be sure to get in immediately the doors opened and get to the toy stand before anyone else.

Maureen was first to arrive. It was just twenty to two by the Village Hall clock. But then she stood and stared! There was a long queue of people spreading right along the pavement outside. It just couldn't be for the jumble sale! But it was! Maybe she could slip in near the front when nobody was looking.

'Now child, what do you think you're doing? Back to the end of the queue, *if* you don't mind,' a cross looking woman wearing a head scarf and carrying two huge shopping bags glared at her.

'That's right, no queue jumping here,' agreed another woman behind the first one.

As Maureen ran back to the end she found the queue had grown longer already. Hilary and Joan had just arrived.

'We'll never get in in time,' wailed Joan, 'look at all those people.'

It seemed an age to wait but promptly at 2 o'clock the queue began to move. At last they were through the door. They pushed their way through the people crowded around the tables loaded with old clothes, shoes and hats. They were jostled and poked and shoved, and when they did manage to reach a trestle table there wasn't a doll or toy to be seen.

'Are there any toys please?' asked Maureen of a flustered looking assistant.

'In the other room.' She pointed to the far end of the hall.

They made their way towards it. Children and grown ups were massing around the tables covered with old toys, games and books.

Hilary asked the girl who was helping if she had a doll with a bandaged leg and one green earring and golden hair. She described Charlotte Anne very clearly. But the girl looked blank and shook her head.

'Haven't seen one like that, there were a lot of dolls but —'

'I saw that one,' interrupted a lady assistant beside her, 'I'm sure I saw it, but it's been bought already, I sold it not long ago.'

'Are you sure?' asked Maureen. 'It's terribly important.'

'Pretty sure,' she smiled. 'Dolls go quickly, sorry.'

The three of them turned away. It was too late.

They made their way out through the people into the sunlit street. Another queue was moving in through the main door. Some people who had got in first were already leaving, shopping bags bulging with purchases.

The Brownies walked gloomily along Market Street, kicking at loose stones on the pavement and trying to look as if they didn't care about having failed. They weren't talking as they turned into the quiet side road that led towards home. A solitary figure, an elderly woman, was walking ahead of them, using a stick. She was small and bent and carried a shopping bag and a handbag on her left arm. Something was sticking out of the bag. It was Hilary who raised her eyes from the pavement and first saw it. A doll! A doll that looked remarkably like Charlotte Anne! As they drew nearer and caught up with the slow moving figure she saw that it *was* Charlotte Anne! The three of them recognised the person who was carrying her at the same moment.

'Mrs Taylor!' they shouted, surrounding the surprised and delighted old lady. To her astonishment Maureen snatched the doll out of her bag and hugged it!

'Found, found and saved!' she chanted, 'Charlotte Anne is safe!'

'What's all this about?' Mrs Taylor stared at the three of them. 'Is it *your* doll?'

'In a way, but it's really Brown Owl's,' Joan started to explain. She and Hilary took the shopping bag and carried it between them while Maureen carried the doll. They were all talking together so Mrs Taylor said they had better come home with her so that she could hear the whole story, and one at a time please.

They took it in turns to tell her the story as they walked along. Maureen started, prompted by the others, and when she reached the point where the doll was found, Hilary continued by telling Mrs Taylor that they did find her note asking them to make a map and that she had finished it. Joan wanted to tell what happened when the map was being made, but by that time they had reached number 7 Manor Square.

In the living-room Mrs Taylor told them it was

her turn to speak now. They put down the shopping bag and waited.

'I've got a surprise for you.' Her cheerful face creased into a twinkling smile, 'and when you know what it is you'll begin to understand just why I was first in the queue for the jumble sale this morning.'

She beckoned them to follow her to a door leading off the hall and opened it wide. The three Brownies stared in amazement at what they saw there.

Chapter 13

It was a small bedroom, and sitting or lying on the bed and on shelves above it were dolls of all description. Baby dolls, boy or girl dolls, and grown up dolls. Most of them were different from the dolls the Brownies were familiar with. They had old-fashioned clothes with lace and frills, ruffles and flounces. Some had china heads and pink cheeks, others were rag dolls with embroidered faces, and one was even carved from wood.

'You may look at them all,' said Mrs Taylor, 'but handle them carefully because some are very fragile.'

'This is like Charlotte Anne,' exclaimed Joan, holding up a golden haired lady doll wearing a long, tight waisted dress with wide sleeves at the shoulders and tiny buttons covered with the same pink material as the dress.

'Yes, I think it's about the same age -70-80 years old. As soon as I saw your doll at the sale I knew it was very old and I bought it to add to the collection, but of course your Brown Owl must have it back, I wouldn't keep it now.'

'Did you buy them all?' breathed Maureen in wonder.

Mrs Taylor laughed.

'No, I've been left the collection by a distant relative of mine who died. She had them in glass cases in the big house where she lived. Of course they're not meant to be played with, they're much too old. But I've only got a tiny house and one glass cabinet so what can I do with them except keep them here while I decide? Of course I could give them away to a museum, but I don't want to part with them. Quite a lot of them need to be

repaired,' she went on, 'and I was lucky enough to get some pieces of material and some beads and lace at the jumble sale that will do beautifully.' She rummaged in the bottom of the shopping bag and brought out a handful of oddments. Opening a paper bag she poured a selection of beads on to her hand. 'Look!' A tiny green glass one sparkled amongst the others. 'I do believe this would match your Charlotte Anne's missing earring.' She placed the bead against the green earring in the doll's left ear. 'Perfect, that's a bit of good luck! I'll attach it if you like before I return the doll to Miss Atkins.'

They decided to leave Charlotte Anne with Mrs Taylor until they could tell Brown Owl the good news next week.

Of course as soon as Brown Owl heard what had happened she called to see Mrs Taylor and spent a long time talking to her and looking at the wonderful collection of dolls. At Pack Meeting that week she told all the Brownies about it, and said that Mrs Taylor would like all the pack to come to see the dolls, a few at a time, as soon as she had repaired the shabbiest ones. She was going to repair Charlotte Anne, too, and the doll would remain with her for the present, there were some plans being made which she couldn't reveal just yet!

She told them some more exciting news too.

'There's going to be a fun fair in the big field next to the Manor very soon, Saturday 17th. Colonel Atkins is going to help run the miniature railway and there'll be a roundabout and all the usual side shows, and a Big Wheel, so I hope you'll all come. Some of the money is going to help handicapped children.'

The Brownies cheered and Maureen gave an inward squeal of delight. She had never been on a Big Wheel and this was her chance to have a first go.

The herb garden was beginning to look like a real garden at last. All the nettles and weeds had gone, revealing paths winding between the flowerbeds. Even Mary was enjoying working on her special bed bordered with pinks and had discovered several kinds of herbs growing there. Soon the Colonel was to make a proper opening into the garden from the shrubbery. Entering by the holes in the hedge was forbidden until he could make an entrance for the people of Manor Square there too, which the Brownies could use.

There was only one thing worrying Maureen and Joan. They looked with envy at the crossed semaphore flags on the badge on Hilary's right arm. Would they ever gain it? The challenge was turning out more difficult than they thought. Mrs

Taylor wrote her shopping lists in semaphore again to help them.

'I can read the words all right,' Maureen admitted, 'but I get mixed up when I signal. Joan can signal better than me but she isn't so good at reading messages.'

'You must never give up,' said Mrs Taylor, 'you'll have those badges before long, I know you will. Keep on practising.' She smiled and took up the little satin dress she was making for one of the dolls and continued sewing a sleeve.

One Saturday morning not long afterwards the village of Ferndale was astir early. The sounds of gay fair organ music thumping out, traction engines whistling and voices shouting drifted across the fields. Soon children and grown ups were leaving their houses and making in the direction of the sound. Peggy and Pat leapfrogged all the way down the garden path and joined the crowds on the way to the fairground. In Market Street they met Valerie, already sucking a lolly.

'I'm going on the Big Wheel with Maureen,' she said, 'and the roundabout.'

Peggy took some money out of her pocket.

'It costs too much to go on everything, but we're going on the miniature railway first.'

They mingled with the crowds streaming in at the entrance. Ahead of them they could see the

miniature railway chugging along. It stopped at
the tiny platform where Colonel Atkins was
taking the money. Another man was driving the
train. Peggy and Pat queued up for a ride and
Valerie ran off to have a look at the Big Wheel.
There it was, slowly revolving against the clear
blue of the summer sky. She had promised to wait
for Maureen and as she stood gazing up at it, the
wheel began to slow down for the end of the ride.
She felt a poke in her back and turned round to
find Maureen and Joan.

'We've been on the roundabout, it's a super
one,' said Joan.

'Let's go on the wheel now, come on,' Valerie
started towards it.

'I don't want to,' Joan hung back.

Maureen suddenly felt undecided too. It did look huge, and she had never tried it before. But Valerie was pulling her towards the pay desk and before she knew what was happening they were climbing into their seats and slowly rising into the air as the other seats were lowered for more people to get in.

They were off! The wheel was moving faster. Up and up they went, like birds soaring into the sky. Now they were at the topmost point of the circle. Now they were coming down. Maureen shut her eyes and squeezed the safety bar in front while people screamed and she felt as if her tummy was left behind, but already the feeling vanished and they were on the way up again.

She opened her eyes. The fairground far below was a blur of colour and sound. The blur resolved itself into shapes of people and canopies and the painted top of the roundabout. They were slowing down! Could the ride be over already? Just as their 'car' was at the highest point of the circle the wheel stopped moving.

'What's happened?' cried Maureen.

Valerie craned her neck over the side.

'Something's up, we're stuck!'

'Will we have to stay up here?' asked Maureen in dismay.

'Suppose so, if it doesn't move,' said Valerie calmly. After a few moments she pulled a lollipop out of her pocket and began to suck it, 'I don't mind.'

Maureen looked over the side. She could see a cluster of men working at the machinery and then she saw the top of Colonel Atkins' white head striding over the grass towards the wheel. When the Colonel was in command everything was sure to be all right, he'd know what to do. She sat back in her seat and drew a deep breath. It was exciting up here really, you could see everything and everybody from a bird's eye view.

There was Joan, a small figure staring up at them. Valerie and Maureen waved and Joan waved back. From here they could even see the houses in Manor Square, and the Manor itself with the broad gravel drive leading to the halldoor, and the high hedge behind which lay the herb garden.

As they looked they saw a figure walking up the drive of the Manor.

'That looks like Miss McNab,' said Maureen.

'It *is* her,' Valerie stared, 'wonder what she's going to the Manor for, she never visits anyone.'

Suddenly Maureen jerked in her seat and grabbed Valerie's arm.

'She's fallen!'

Miss McNab lay by the side of the drive and she

wasn't getting up. She sat up, holding her leg. She tried to stand up but couldn't and sat down again.

'Joan,' screamed Valerie, cupping her hands over her mouth, 'Miss McNab's fallen in the Manor drive, over there,' she pointed.

Joan looked blank, glancing over her shoulder. She couldn't hear a word.

'It's no good, she can't hear,' cried Maureen.

Looking down, Maureen saw Colonel Atkins smiling and waving up as if to re-assure them.

Then he nodded. That meant they'd be off again soon.

'What'll we do?' she moaned.

'Signal a message to Joan,' said Valerie calmly, 'you're learning semaphore, signal, hurry up, we might move soon!'

Maureen thought quickly. She'd have to signal without flags and sitting down, and what was she going to say?

'Say, "Accident at Manor"' suggested Valerie.

Maureen waved her arms up and down to attract Joan's attention and began to signal the letter 'A'. The message would have to be right. There would be no time to signal 'E' eight times now, just no time at all!

Chapter 14

'How do you spell it?' gasped Maureen after she had signalled

 and

'Two C's I think'. Valerie kept calling out the letters while Maureen signalled them.

Joan was watching closely.

'Oh good, semaphore practice,' she thought.

Maureen tried to signal slowly and evenly in spite of a pounding heart. It would be no good if Joan couldn't read it.

She lowered her arms after the final letter:-

To her relief Joan signalled 'C' to show she understood. Joan's face grew pink with excitement. There really was an accident! That's what Valerie had been shouting and pointing about! But here came the next word.

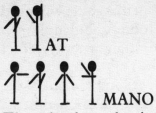AT

MANO

The wheel was beginning to move. As Maureen and Valerie floated down towards her Joan saw Maureen with arms outstretched

'R'. An easy one.

'Accident at Manor'. What should she do? Grown up help. Plenty of people about, but who? Then she remembered. Turning, she ran as fast as she had ever done in the direction of the St. John Ambulance Brigade tent. It was right in the middle of the fairground, she had seen it earlier.

A few minutes later Miss McNab was being lifted on to a stretcher.

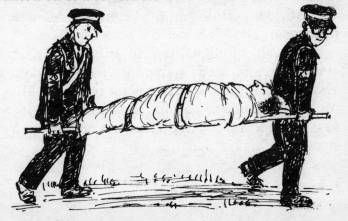

'You'll be all right now, but that ankle will need to be X-rayed,' said the St John Ambulance man, 'we'll get you to hospital straight away, don't worry.'

Miss McNab opened her eyes and saw one of the children who visited her. Yes, she remembered her name was Joan. What was she doing here? It was all very confusing but now the nightmare was over and she was being looked after.

As the ambulance drove away Joan saw the Colonel hurrying up the drive.

'There's been an accident, Miss McNab fell,' she said.

'I know. I followed the St John Ambulance people as soon as I could,' he panted. 'I read that semaphore message, you didn't know of course. Get Maureen as soon as she comes down off the big wheel, I want to speak to you both.'

Back at the fair ground they found Maureen and Valerie having a fizzy drink at a refreshment kiosk. The world was still spinning slightly for Maureen but already she felt better.

'Fine bit of signalling in difficult circumstances,' announced Colonel Atkins. 'Well done, I was watching and read the message myself. Miss McNab has gone to hospital, hurt her ankle, Joan says. She'll be all right now, thanks to you Brownies.'

'I helped by spelling it for Maureen,' said Valerie.

'Excellent, excellent, you must learn semaphore yourself now. I can tell Joan and Maureen,' he boomed, 'they've passed Signaller Badge with full marks, full marks!'

Miss McNab was to stay in hospital for a day or two. Her ankle was bandaged but with no serious damage done. She would be home again as soon as she recovered from the shock. Brown Owl told the Brownies when she 'phoned the hospital. She had been in another part of the fairground when the big wheel stuck, but had heard all about it from the Colonel.

'I'm really proud of the three of you,' she said. 'Miss McNab would have been lying there longer if you hadn't been quick enough to see her and to signal so well. I wonder why she was going to call at the Manor?

'Can we visit her and find out?' asked Maureen.

'And bring her something,' suggested Valerie, 'to cheer her up.'

'Let's bring Charlotte Anne,' Maureen had a sudden idea, 'and I can tell her the story.'

'She doesn't like much talking,' warned Joan. 'It makes her head ache.'

Brown Owl said they could go if they promised only to stay a short time and to talk quietly.

The next day they called to collect the doll from Mrs Taylor and tell about the happening at the fair.

'We've passed Signaller Badge,' Maureen gave a skip of joy, 'and Colonel Atkins said we earned it by using semaphore so well in an emergency.'

Mrs Taylor clapped her hands in delight.

'I knew you'd pass, well done, and you've had an adventure while doing it, much more exciting! I've been working on Charlotte Anne, look!' The doll had a completely new leg, and Mrs Taylor was making her a new dress of pale green material to match the green earrings.

'I'll call in to see poor Miss McNab when she comes home from hospital,' she told them, 'she'll need a visitor then.'

The three of them took the bus to the hospital at Bayhurst, carrying Charlotte Anne wrapped in paper in a shopping bag.

Miss McNab was in a ward on the first floor and as they reached the top of the stairs they asked a nurse to direct them.

'Only two visitors allowed at a time,' she smiled, 'but as she's well enough to go home tomorrow the three of you may go in, but don't tire her.'

Miss McNab was sitting up reading a book. Her glasses had slipped down to the end of her nose and she looked more as if she was thinking than reading. She saw them as they approached the bed. The book slipped out of her hands and she smiled, pushing her glasses back in place.

'This is a surprise.'

'We've got a lot to tell you,' said Valerie softly, 'so we thought we'd come today, we'll be very quiet.'

'I remember I saw *you* when the ambulance came,' Miss McNab turned to Joan, 'How did —'

'That's what we've come to tell,' said Joan.

Miss McNab's pale face flushed as the story progressed.

'Well, I never – semaphore! I wouldn't have believed it possible.' She seemed to be seeing the Brownies in a new light and gazed at them in amazement. 'So if the big wheel hadn't stuck and you hadn't seen me I could have been lying there even longer!'

'There's something else to tell,' said Maureen eagerly. Valerie poked her and she lowered her voice. 'It happened when we were practising semaphore for the badge, at the Manor. It was my turn.' As she went on something very astonishing happened. Miss McNab sat bolt upright, clutching the bedclothes. She was breathing heavily and her eyes were bright.

'Are you all right?' asked Joan anxiously. 'Do you want us to go away?'

'Go on,' said Miss McNab to Maureen.

'So I put my hand in, it was all spidery down there but I didn't mind. I felt something, not a spider, but something big, it felt like a doll. I pulled it out, it *was* a doll, it had —'

'It had golden hair and pink cheeks – china – two green earrings and a long dress, in pink,' interrupted the old lady.

'One green earring,' Maureen corrected. 'How did you know?'

'Because it belonged to me,' said Miss McNab, 'it belonged to me.'

Chapter 15

Maureen placed the doll in Miss McNab's trembling hands.

'Anne!' exclaimed the old lady, 'it just can't be true! After all these years! And she *has* two green earrings!'

'Mrs Taylor gave her a new one to match. She has a collection of dolls now and she's mending them, she's given Charlotte Anne a new leg too.' said Maureen.

'*Charlotte* Anne did you say?' asked Miss McNab.

'M-mm,' replied Joan, 'we went to the church to see if we could find the name of someone living in the Manor about 1910, who might have owned her. We looked at the record books, and there was a girl called Charlotte Anne. Her parents died.'

'I know,' said the old lady, 'and I'll tell you the whole story. Listen carefully and don't interrupt.

'When I was your age, my parents lived in Ferndale. I made a friend, a daughter of the Adams

family who lived in the Manor at that time. Her name was Charlotte Anne, and she had a younger brother called James. I often went to play with her, we both loved dolls, and she had lots of them. But my parents weren't well off and I only had a few. Anne was my favourite, I called her that after my friend's second name. We had wonderful games with them. We used to play in a herb garden near the stables.'

Maureen opened her mouth to speak but stopped in time as Miss McNab continued.

'Charlotte's brother, James, always spoilt our games. He *was* a nuisance. Jealous, I expect, he hadn't any brothers or friends to play with, poor child! Then came the sad day when Charlotte's mother died. They had a kind housekeeper, and I still went to play there, but a year later came the war in 1914 and Charlotte's father went away to fight in it.

'One day I lost my doll, Anne. I was sure I had left her in a certain room at the Manor, but she wasn't there. Charlotte and I hunted everywhere but she had vanished. I thought someone had stolen her. A day or two later came the news that poor Charlotte's father had been killed in the war. She and James went to live with relatives, and I never saw the doll again, until today!'

'How did she get under the floor?' asked Joan.

'Charlotte and I always kept in touch, we wrote to each other, even after we were grown up and she married and went to live in another part of the country. In her last letter she told me that her brother James told her he had once hidden a doll of mine as a joke under some loose boards in the playroom. He forgot all about it when the news of his father's death came, and they went away. He asked her did I ever find it? Of course I hadn't.

'I thought if I called on Miss Atkins and her father they would think me a very silly old woman to worry about the loss of a doll years ago. But I did long to see Anne again, and I decided, as I now lived so near the Manor, to call there and tell Miss Atkins the whole story. But I forgot everyone would be at the fair, and then I twisted my ankle on the drive.'

'Poor Miss McNab,' said Maureen softly, stroking her hand, 'you can have Anne back now, she's yours, just like when you were a little girl.'

The bell clanged for the end of visiting hour and Miss McNab looked so pale after all the talking that they whispered goodbye and stole away without saying another word.

But when they went to visit her at home a few days later they found something wonderful had happened. She was sitting in a chair, her ankle bandaged but her face smiling and happy. She looked so different that for a moment they could only stare. Her cheeks glowed and her eyes were smiling, and in spite of her nose she hardly looked like a hawk at all! Mrs Taylor was there and the two ladies were surrounded by a selection of the dolls, Charlotte Anne (or Anne as she was now called) in the middle of them.

'My friend Miss McNab is helping me restore the dolls,' Mrs Taylor told them delightedly. 'Her doll, Anne, is almost finished.'

'Look in the doll's trunk,' said Miss McNab,

pointing to the little travelling trunk they had
noticed the day the budgie escaped and was perching on it. The lid was open and it lay on a table.
Inside was a selection of Anne's clothes; a lace
trimmed petticoat, stockings, and a hat. The three
Brownies held them up and admired them all.

'I've got another bit of good news,' Mrs Taylor
told them. 'Miss Atkins and her father have
obtained an empty shop in the village for me
where I'm going to have a doll museum. The pro-
ceeds will go to help handicapped children, and

Miss McNab is going to help me run it!'

'It's been a super Venture,' said Joan at Pack meeting that week.

'We didn't know it was going to be so exciting when it started,' agreed Maureen.

'Oh, is it over?' asked Valerie sadly.

'It needn't be,' said Brown Owl, 'I'm sure you could go on helping at Manor Square.'

'They'd miss us now if we didn't,' said Mary, 'Mrs Hamilton likes me coming and talking and telling her everything.'

'Remember how it all started,' said Hilary, 'I asked you to meet under the tree and think of an idea for a Venture then —'

'And then I stood on my head and saw the message when I was upside down,' said Pat.

She knelt down, placed her head on the floor, clasped her arms around it and slowly raised her legs in the air.

'That's great,' said Peggy admiringly.

'Hush!' said Pat, 'I'm thinking.'

If you have enjoyed reading this, why not try some of the Knight books listed on the following pages?

Post·A·Book

A Royal Mail service in association with the Book Marketing Council & The Booksellers Association.

Post-A-Book is a Post Office trademark.

BEAVER TOWERS

NIGEL HINTON

A magic spell whisks Philip away on his new kite to a far-off island, where he meets the beavers, Mr Edgar and his grandson, Baby B.

They tell him of the terrible danger that threatens them all. The wicked witch Oyin has imprisoned most of the island's inhabitants in Beaver Towers, Mr Edgar's old home. As soon as her powers are complete she will put them to death and rule the island.

Only magic can save the animals, and Philip agrees to try to obtain Mr Edgar's vital spell book from right under the witch's nose . . .

KNIGHT BOOKS

THE WITCH'S REVENGE

NIGEL HINTON

In this enchanting sequel to *Beaver Towers*, Philip realises that his old friends the beavers must be in trouble when he sees Mr Edgar's magic cloud hovering outside his bedroom window, so he takes his kite and flies off to their magical island.

The wicked witch Oyin, furious at the failure of her plan to take over Beaver Towers, is plotting her terrifying revenge ...

Using the evil forces of Earth, Air, Fire and Water, it seems as though she will succeed in destroying the island, but the beavers, led by Mr Edgar and his grandson Baby B, have Philip on their side.

KNIGHT BOOKS

THE LITTLE WATER-SPRITE

OTFRIED PREUSSLER

One spring day a little water-sprite was born in a mill pond. Like all true water-sprites he had webbed hands and green eyes and hair.

As soon as he could swim he explored the cool green world of the pond, and was even allowed to visit the world outside, as long as he did not let his feet get dry!

The curious and cheeky little water-sprite had lots of adventures both in and out of the pond. Sometimes his fun and games got him into trouble, but life was always exciting.

KNIGHT BOOKS

PATRICK COMES TO PUTTYVILLE

GEOFFREY HAYES

Patrick is sad when he and Mama Bear leave Catfish Bay and Grandpa Poopdeck behind to move to the country. At first he hates Miss Peckinpaw's Day School – until he makes friends with Ted, another small bear who has recently arrived in Puttyville.

Patrick's first months there are filled with adventure as he learns all sorts of surprising things about his new life. They culminate in a very exciting birthday party, with a special present for Patrick.

KNIGHT BOOKS

KNIGHT BOOKS

Nigel Hinton

☐ 32105 9 *Beaver Towers* £1.10
☐ 32104 0 *Witch's Revenge* £1.25

Otfried Preussler

☐ 28643 1 *The Little Water Sprite* £1.25

Geoffrey Hayes

☐ 25509 9 *Patrick Comes to Puttyville* 70p

All these books are available at your local bookshop or newsagent, or can be ordered direct from the publisher. Just tick the titles you want and fill in the form below.

Prices and availability subject to change without notice.

KNIGHT BOOKS, P.O. Box 11, Falmouth, Cornwall.

Please send cheque or postal order, and allow the following for postage and packing:

U.K. – 55p for one book, plus 22p for the second book, and 14p for each additional book ordered up to a £1.75 maximum.

B.F.P.O. and EIRE – 55p for the first book, plus 22p for the second book, and 14p per copy for the next 7 books, 8p per book thereafter.

OTHER OVERSEAS CUSTOMERS – £1.00 for the first book plus 25p per copy for each additional book.

Name ....

Address...

....